The Hunter's Apprentice

The Ravencrest Chronicles
Book Two

By B.K. Bass

Published in the U.S. by B.K. Bass, 2021
Third Edition

Third Edition, 2021

ISBN: 9798705572960 (print) 9781393019978 (eBook)

Previously published by Kyanite Publishing, 2019
First published by B.K. Bass, 2018

Published by B.K. Bass in the United States of America

Cover and interior art licensed from Dreamstime.com

B.K. Bass can be reached at https://bkbass.com/contact/

For behind the scenes access and the latest news, subscribe to B.K.'s newsletter here: http://eepurl.com/dpaU6f

Visit the author's website at https://bkbass.com

Books by B.K. Bass

<u>The Ravencrest Chronicles</u>
Seahaven
The Hunter's Apprentice
The Giant and the Fishes
Tales from the Lusty Mermaid, a Ravencrest Chronicles Anthology
The Ravencrest Chronicles: Omnibus One
Curse of the Pirate King (The Pirate King Duology: Book One)
Shadow of the Pirate King (The Pirate King Duology: Book Two)

<u>The Night Trilogy</u>
Night Shift
Night Life
Night Shadow

<u>The Tales of Durgan Stoutheart</u>
Warriors of Understone
Companions of the Stone Road (forthcoming)

<u>The Burning Sands</u>
Blood of the Desert
Into the Red Wastes (forthcoming)

<u>Beyond the Veil</u>
Parting the Veil

<u>Standalone Novels</u>
What Once Was Home

Chapter One

Miles padded silently through the shadows of the back alley, his bare feet making nary a sound. Both moons were full tonight, but there was darkness enough in the tight confines of the city streets for him to hide in. He found the door he was looking for and smiled a crooked smile. A few teeth were missing, a reminder to avoid a fight when one could. He crouched down before the door, the knee of his ripped and torn trousers wet in a puddle. He shook his unruly mop of dirty blond hair, blowing a few loose strands away from his eyes. The door had an iron lock set into it, but that would not be a problem for the young thief. Miles reached into a pocket and fished around for his steel picks, which had been a gift from his mentor. He deftly inserted the picks into the lock, feeling for the tumblers and setting them into place one by one. There were four in all, a complicated lock for this part of the city, but in no time, he had the door open. Sliding inside unseen and unheard, he softly pressed the door closed behind him.

The back room of the shop was unremarkable, with stacks of crates and an odd barrel here and there. The smell of salted fish was heavy in the butcher's storeroom, made that much more acute by the smell of smoke from a fire in the next room. There was a brick chimney there that formed a cylinder in the center of the room. At the bottom was a large space for a fire, and above were racks and hooks for smoking meat behind a heavy iron door. The chimney was full of all sorts of mutton, pork, and fish; even at this hour of the night. There would be hungry bellies in Seahaven in the morning, and the butcher was sure to have smoked herring ready for the breakfast rush.

Miles, however, would not wait that long. He found several parchment sheets and bundled the more done-looking pieces of fish from the chimney, adding a few crabs for good measure. He took as much as he could carry, and considering he was an athletic sixteen-year-old, that was a pretty good haul. Filling a burlap sack with the parchment bundles, he headed over to the counter in the next room. This was where Haemish the butcher would greet his customers in a few hours. Below the counter was a small coffer. Miles knew this was not the meat vendor's treasure trove, but the spare coin would be enough. There was a silver piece in there, a few copper coins, and a handful of copper bits. Enough for some drink for everybody, with some to spare.

Miles smiled that crooked smile, his missing teeth making it just that much more charming. His bronzed skin, dark from spending so much time in the summer sun, glistened with sweat as he walked back by the fire and towards the rear door to the shop. Silently he passed through the portal and made his way back down the alley and out to the street. Two-story building surrounded him, almost all of them of daub and wattle construction with cobblestone foundations.

There were a few pieced together with wooden plank, but this was rare.

The sun would rise over Seahaven soon. The predawn glow was visible out towards the harbor district. From where he was on Trader's Way in the Mercantile District, Miles could see all the way down the hill to the ocean. The principal thoroughfare of the city was broad and open, one of the few streets that did not make one feel like they were being smothered by the surrounding buildings. The cobbles of the street were even, smooth, and well maintained. The hill rose sharply from the sea into the Noble Quarter, where the road twisted and turned to make the ascent manageable. In this part of the city there were great stone manors surrounded by protective walls.

In the other direction was the harbor, beyond the sprawl of the city. Trader's Way cut a neat path through the center of it all and looked like a scar dug out of the landscape. All around it were mazes of side streets and back roads lined with shanties, shacks, and hovels. Some homes and businesses were quite nice, and there were even several with log walls instead of plank. But most of them consisted of rough timber and wood planks, with roofs of tree bark shingles or thatch.

It was here in Shanty Town that most of the residents of Seahaven struggled to survive.

Beyond was the harbor itself, lined with docks which hosted an array of sailing ships. There were two-masted schooners bound for local ports, three-masted carracks ready to travel abroad, and even strange caravels and galleys from faraway lands. All there for the one thing that made Seahaven more than just another fishing village on the coast: coin. Seahaven was a trade port. Goods and coin flowed into and out of the city daily. Most of the people of Seahaven, though they might labor at one enterprise or another, never saw much of that coin.

Up the hill it went, and the aristocracy hoarded most of it there. The middle-class merchants ended up with a comfortable share, but even their fat bellies and jingly purses paled compared to the coffers of the Noble Quarter. Beyond that, atop one of the two soaring cliffs that bracket the city and Bleakstone Bay, sat Castle Ravencrest. This was the home of the so-called lord of Seahaven, Duke Piotr. He rarely made public appearances, leaving the bureaucracy of the city to the Council of Barons. And thus had life in Seahaven always been, and so it would always be. Miles sighed as he looked up at the castle on the bluff, wondering what it was like inside. *Maybe one day I'll break in and rob the place*, he thought. Laughing at the notion, he continued to make his way down into Shanty Town.

The sun had peeked over the horizon and he could hear the gulls crying their morning calls. The sea sparkled green and blue under the light, and long shadows from the masts of sailing ships drew lines over Shanty Town. Miles came down the hill to the clustered shacks he called home, and the shadows between them soon sheltered him. He wove his way along the twisting alleys, cobbled streets giving way to packed dirt. The people of Shanty Town were rising with the sun, and he usually got a wave and a smile as he passed by. The city of Seahaven was large, and nobody could know every soul within its stone walls, but Miles was close to home and the community here was tightly knit. He waved to Loden, the blacksmith, as he pivoted down a narrow path between his shop and the next building. He tossed the sack down next to a large bale of hay and pulled a filet of smoked fish from a bundle of parchment. He jumped on top of the hay and nibbled at the fish, savoring the smoky and salty flavors. The hay was there for Nance, who was Loden's donkey. Nance's job was to walk in a circle, turning a large wheel attached to the blacksmith's bellows. It was a marvelous contraption that saved Loden and his apprentices time and effort and kept the fires of the forge hot all-day long. In return, there was always fresh hay and carrots for Nance. Loden kept the carrots inside, though.

Loden tolerated having Miles living in the alley behind his shop, and in return Miles kept an eye out for the blacksmith and drove off any would-be thieves. Sure, Miles was a thief, but he didn't steal from Loden, and that was all that concerned the burly blacksmith. Miles had been living on the streets for almost five years, since his ma and pa mysteriously disappeared. That happened a lot in Seahaven, especially to the poor. People would go about their business one day, and the next they would vanish.

Miles could have gone to stay at the orphanage with Helen, but he liked it out here on the streets. He wasn't much of a people person, except for a close group of friends, so the mere thought of being in the big house with all those brats made him queasy. He would rather be on his own, make his own rules, and find his own way. He did well for himself, truth be told. He was rarely hungry and often had a few coins jingling around in his pocket. Much of this was due to his intrepid enterprises like this morning's trip to the meat market, and much of it was due to his shadowy benefactor.

Miles was a sparrow.

One might hear that word and imagine an insignificant creature that flits about silently. They might think of something that cocks its head, watching and listening, and that takes flight at the first sign of trouble. A tiny thing that, in the right moment, may chirp and sing for you. If they were thinking about a bird, they would be wrong.

Miles was a sparrow, as were many of his friends. Street urchins and poor waifs—every one of them—the sparrows were the eyes and ears of the most renowned thief in all of Seahaven: Gareth Vann. They would hide in plain sight, watching and listening. Their hungry eyes ensured that nobody with half a copper looked at them, lest they feel the pang of guilt at not helping the poor soul. They were dirty little scoundrels, skilled at a variety of nefarious tasks.

Gareth would come with sausages, biscuits, pastries, and coin. He would ask them, "Little sparrow, what's new today?" And so, his birds would sing to him; and he would know who had been where, with whom, and what they were doing. And if there were coin changing hands, or goods being smuggled,

Gareth knew about it; because the sparrows saw it happen or heard that it was about to.

Miles was not only a sparrow, he was one of the oldest. He had known Gareth for a few years now, but in the last several months the man had taught him more and more of the shadow craft. He had given him the picks and taught him their use. He had even given Miles a small dirk, barely a hand span long, to defend himself with. He always had it with him, in a battered sheath hidden under his baggy shirt.

The shadows were shortening as the sun rose, and it surprised Miles that none of the other sparrows had stopped by yet. They knew he had been planning to gather food, so they should show up. Just as he was thinking this, the first of them rounded the corner. Naturally, it was Nathan. The burly young man was the same age as Miles, but had twice the appetite. They were the same height, but Nathan was broad of stature and heavily muscled, while Miles was lithe and agile. His friend was the thug of the bunch, and although he was not as discreet as the other sparrows, he had his uses when somebody needed their skull thumped.

"Nathan, good morrow!" Miles called out, reaching into the sack and throwing a parchment wrapped bundle of fish to the other boy.

Nathan struggled clumsily to catch the bundle, cursing under his breath, and shot an annoyed glare at Miles. "Could have just handed it to me, you little bugger."

"No fun in that. How would I get to see you flailing about like your breakfast did when it was pulled into the boat?" Miles was laughing so hard he had to hold his belly.

Nathan shoved an entire fillet in his mouth and said, "I gmph mphk mur amphs." Bits of flaky fish fell out of his mouth, sticking to his puffy lips. He smiled, showing off even more of his half-eaten breakfast.

"Gross, tell him to stop," a girl said.

Miles looked over and there was Hatha, standing right next to him. He would swear that even if he had been looking, she still would have sneaked up on him. The little curly-haired blond with blue eyes could stand out in a crowd if she wanted to, or she could creep up on a door mouse without being heard. Either way, she made for the perfect cutpurse. Either you saw her and thought she was too adorable to do any harm, or you never even knew she was there.

"Okay, Nathan, that's enough," Miles admonished his friend.

Nathan wiped his mouth with the back of his arm and said to Hatha, "I'm sorry."

Just then, Miles heard a crunching noise and looked down from the hay bale to see Liam standing over his bag, cracking open one of the smoked crabs. "When did you get here?"

The bronze skinned child shrugged his shoulders and stuffed a bit of crab meat into his mouth. His dark skin and tight, curly hair stood in testament to Liam's southern origins. His parents had probably come to Seahaven hoping to make their fortune. His presence in the alley spoke of their success at that endeavor. The boy was an exceptional sneak, and this was not the first time he had surprised Miles like this. The young boy said little, but when he spoke, it was usually worth listening.

"Well," a gruff voice said, "looks like you're all eating well this morning."

Miles looked up and saw his friend and mentor, Gareth Vann, strolling down the alley. The man was in his thirties and maintained an exemplary physique. He wore his trademark dark cloak, jacket, pants, and knee-high boots. The hilts of daggers peeked out from his coat, along with a short bow and a quiver of arrows hanging at his hip. Miles knew as well that there was a sword beneath the man's cloak, carved of gleaming black obsidian and razor sharp. Gareth did not use it often, and he talked about it less. He rubbed his square chin covered in dark stubble and said, "I don't suppose you have any more of that smoked fish?"

Miles smiled up at his old friend. "Well, isn't this a change? Usually we're having to tell you the news to get food from you. Now you're hoping for a handout?" They all laughed at the irony except Liam, who remained quiet as usual.

"How about a trade?" Gareth asked, producing a cloth-wrapped bundle. He opened it, revealing some sticky sweet rolls. They had surely come from Helen's kitchens at the orphanage. The eyes of the sparrows widened. They all knew how good Helen's sweet rolls were.

"Deal!" Nathan said.

"Dammit, Nathan, who taught you how to haggle?" Miles said.

"Obviously, not me," Gareth replied, smiling as he handed over the pastries and took his fish. "You've been doing well for yourself, I see."

Miles sat up straight, trying to look taller and prouder than usual. "Of course, I'm a master thief."

Again, there was a round of laughter from the sparrows. This time even Liam chuckled softly.

"Sure, you are," Gareth chided, "and I'm the master of the seas. Come on, we have business."

Miles glared at the others, who quickly silenced their mirth. "See? Business. He needs help from the master thief."

Chapter Two

Miles looked down at his wrinkled and sore hands. He had been scrubbing pots in the orphanage's kitchen for what felt like hours. "I thought you said we had business?"

Seated by the cooking fires, Gareth had his feet propped up on a table and a pipe in his mouth. He took a long puff of smoke and exhaled slowly. "We did."

"This?" Miles asked, gesturing at the basin full of iron pots.

"Yes," Gareth said. "It's always good to help a friend..."

"Because you never know when you might need their help," Miles repeated the lesson from memory. Gareth had been teaching him a lot of exciting things about being a master thief. This, apparently, was one of the less exciting parts of a life in the shadows. He didn't mind too much, because he was sure that Helen would feed him well in return for the work. It was getting close to dinnertime, and his belly rumbled, reminding him he had more to do. "Why don't you give me a hand? We'll finish faster."

Gareth smiled and scratched at the stubble on his cheek. "You won't gain Helen's favor as quickly if I do half the work. Some honest work builds character, anyway."

"Honest work? We are thieves. Why should we worry about all of that?"

"Because, young man," a shaky female voice replied, "there is a difference between a scoundrel and a villain. Listen to Gareth. He may not make you wealthy, but he knows what he is talking about."

Miles glared as Gareth smiled at Helen. The old woman ran the orphanage and had raised Gareth in these same walls. She had not taught him the shadow craft, though. The bragging rights to that feat belonged to a man named Kholas, who was now probably out on the sea somewhere attacking some hapless merchantman and stealing his cargo. Kholas used to live the life that Gareth now lives and had taught him, just as Gareth was now teaching Miles. The older man, however, had decided on the life of a pirate by the time he was the age that Gareth is now.

"You're too kind, Helen," Gareth said.

"No," she admonished. "I am simply telling the young man the truth. I've tried to get him to come live here with me, but he prefers the streets. At least you can teach him how to survive out there."

"I know how to survive," Miles spoke up.

Both Gareth and Helen shot him disapproving glares, but this time it was Gareth who spoke, "All and well, little thief, but there is much more for you to learn than you can even imagine." With this, Helen squeezed Gareth's shoulder. She was glaring at the man, shaking her head slightly. It seemed to Miles that the two were having some unspoken conversation, and they were not agreeing with each other.

"Regardless," Helen broke the silence. "It is nearly dinner time. Julla should have the stew ready by now, so you two wash up. Miles, you can gather the children for dinner and save me the trouble, if you'll be a dear."

Miles nodded and eagerly set about scrubbing the grease from his hands and arms. He took off at almost a run through the old cobblestone building, grabbing the corner of plastered walls to make turns at speed. He may not have lived in the orphanage, but he knew the place well. Gareth had brought him here often, and he had done work for food. The other children had to work as well, and learned that despite how lucky they were, nothing in life was free.

The orphanage was a large building and had in-fact been a successful inn some years ago. Rumor was, Helen's father was the innkeeper, and when he died and left her the deed, she turned the place toward more altruistic pursuits. Now, the spacious rooms of the old inn housed children who would have otherwise been homeless. These orphans worked to keep their own home clean in exchange for the privilege, and Helen kept them to exacting standards. Miles found many of them still at their chores, but they happily abandoned any task upon hearing that supper was ready.

Returning to the common room with a small army of ragged children in tow, Miles saw the orphanage's cook, Julla, pushing a wood cart topped with an iron pot. Steam and the most wonderful aroma rose from the vessel. Miles could guess what was inside from the smell. He could detect onion, garlic, carrots, potatoes, leeks, crab, and shrimp. Piled atop the cart next to the pot were several loaves of freshly baked bread. The children of the orphanage always ate well, and Miles knew it was in no small part thanks to Gareth. For every ten pieces of silver Gareth stole, Miles was sure that at least seven went to Helen.

*   *   *

After the evening meal, Miles and Gareth said their goodbyes and headed out onto the darkened streets of Seahaven. They were both in cheerful moods, and Miles was enjoying the casual stroll with his old friend. The hustle and bustle of the city streets was dwindling, even in this part of the Mercantile District. Shopkeepers were shuttering their windows and locking their doors. They had loaded produce and other sundry goods found in the markets from the stalls onto wagons, and from there to storerooms and basements throughout the area. A few clouds flitted across the sky, obscuring the two shining moons slightly from time to time. The shadows were fickle this night.

"See how the light comes and goes with the clouds?" Gareth asked.

Miles nodded.

"Always watch the shadows move before you do. A place that might seem hidden in the darkness one moment may be lit up like the dawn the next. Always make sure where you are hiding is in the deep shadows."

"I know all of this," Miles complained. He had heard these lessons time and time again.

"You are impatient, and that will get you killed."

"Why don't I show you that I know what I'm doing?"

Gareth thought on this a moment, then looked around the deserted cobblestone streets. There was nary a soul about, but it was still too early for them to be soundly sleeping. He knew one old lout, though, that ought to be firmly snoring by now. "Fine, follow me."

Miles followed as closely as he could while Gareth leaped atop barrels and grappled onto beams and ropes. The more experienced thief was soon on the rooftops, his favorite place to walk. Miles struggled to catch up, dragging himself from one landing to the next with not half the grace as his teacher. Finally, though, he was atop the clay-tiled roofs and running to catch Gareth. They ran, jumped, and climbed like this for quite a while. Miles thought maybe Gareth was leading them in circles, trying to wear him out. He had plenty of energy, though, and was doing well to keep up.

Gareth came to the edge of a building and stopped, holding a hand out for Miles to do likewise. He pointed at a building across the street, connected by a handy rope run between the edifices for hanging flags during festivals. "That balcony there, on the second floor. See what you can find in there."

Miles looked. It was an unassuming building, much like many others in this neighborhood. There was a small storefront, and above the door a sign painted with a toy soldier on it. Shutters covered the ground-floor windows, but the second-floor window was bare. "The toy carver?"

"One and the same. You've heard of his prices, he is sure to have ample coin," Gareth said, smiling.

"Fine," Miles said. "I'll be back in a jiff, and you'll see that I've got this figured out."

Miles lowered himself from the roof slowly, grabbing onto the rope. He moved along it hand-over-hand until he reached the balcony, then dropped down. The window opened easily enough, and he crept inside. The room he entered was a bedroom, and the occupant seemed to snore contentedly. There were shelves filled with carved wooden toys, but no coffer to be seen. Miles rummaged through the man's wardrobe, vanity, and even a chest at the foot of his bed. He found clothes, dirty clothes, and some scraps of parchment. He was about to go through the door into the hall when a voice startled him.

"I wouldn't open that door, if I were you."

Miles turned to see that the man who had been snoring moments before was now standing by the bed. He was a chubby fellow, middle-aged, with a halo of gray hair and mutton chops that matched.

"And why is that?" Miles said.

"Obstinate, isn't he?" the man asked, looking over his shoulder.

"You really just figured that out, Brachus?" Gareth was sitting on the windowsill, pipe in hand. He puffed on the tobacco in the pipe twice, then blew it out into the night air.

"Must you smoke that in here?" Brachus asked.

"I'm not in here, my friend. I'm mostly out there," Gareth said, gesturing out into the night with the pipe.

Miles stood there in shock. He knew Gareth had robbed the toy maker in the past. To see them talking like old friends was shocking. "What in the seven hells, Gareth?" he demanded.

Both older men laughed. Brachus sat on the edge of his bed, lighting some candles. Gareth puffed on his pipe again, then said, "Miles, meet Brachus. We go way back."

"Yeah, you've been trying to rob me blind for years," Brachus said.

"True, at that. But now we are good friends." Gareth took on an ominous tone. "Miles, if you are ever in trouble, you can come to Brachus. He will help you, no matter what."

"You said that about Jacob, too," Miles said, referring to the proprietor of the Lusty Mermaid tavern and inn.

Gareth nodded. "Yes, him too. And Helen, of course. Although, either Brachus or Jacob may offer more... proactive solutions than she."

Brachus set down the candle he had lit, then walked over to Miles and laid a hand on his shoulder. "Miles, you may feel alone at times out there, but remember that you are not. Some of us know much of what happens in the shadows, and we want to help."

"Brachus and Jacob are among them, but there's more. You'll meet them eventually," Gareth said.

Just then, there was a whistle from down in the street. Gareth's head pivoted, one hand reaching for the sword behind his back. Miles ran over to the window and saw a man down in the street. He was tall and slender, clothed in the hooded cloak and dark attire of a thief. He was waving up at Gareth, who called down, "Filian, what is it?"

"Trouble in Old Town," Filian replied from the street, referring to a part of the city which most had abandoned long ago. Old Town was where the first settlers had built their homes in what would eventually be the city of Seahaven. Nestled under the foot of the cliff that held Castle Ravencrest, this part of the city was home only to the most desperate denizens. The buildings there were mostly roughhewn stone, many of which had timber roofs that had rotted away long ago. The cliffs, the harbor, and one of the poorer parts of Shanty Town penned in the area. People rarely went into Old Town. There were stories of people disappearing, or worse. Trouble there, Miles thought, did not seem out of the ordinary.

Chapter Three

Miles walked along beside Gareth and Filian. The two of them had been acquaintances for a long time. They worked together occasionally, teaming up on some heist or another. When one was in trouble, they knew they could rely on each other for aid. Miles had met Filian on one such occasion. The skinny, hawk-nosed thief had run into trouble with some sailors. They had not taken kindly to him besting them at a game of dice. He had asked Gareth for help, and Gareth had brought Miles along. Together, the three of them had convinced the sailors that not only were Filian's dice not shaved, but that questioning his integrity was a sure way to a broken nose. Of course, Filian shaved his dice—and loaded them—but that was beside the point.

Miles listened as the two men reminisced about some of their old escapades. Most of the stories ran along similar lines as the one with the dice. Filian tried to cheat somebody and got in over his head, then Gareth bailed him out. There were some variations, like Filian helping Gareth with some complicated scam. Other times Filian had somebody that needed shaken down, and Gareth's imposing presence aided in such endeavors. One time, they had even beaten up a pimp who was threatening the prostitutes in the Harbor District. Filian said something about Gareth being out 'chasing shadows' that night, but Miles didn't get the reference.

There was a lot about Gareth that Miles didn't understand. This was surprising, since they had spent a lot of time together lately. It all started about two years ago, when Gareth was having some sort of problem. He had survived whatever the ordeal was, but he had come out of it beaten worse than a man with a bad gambling debt. After, his entire attitude changed. Gareth had been a mostly cheerful fellow. He always drank a lot, and sometimes he was far too intense. But since that time, the man's intensity had become the most prominent part of his personality. This was about the time he got that obsidian sword that he kept hidden under his cloak. Shortly after, he took to carrying a bow as well. Before all of this, he usually only carried a stiletto in his boot.

Now, there was this talk of trouble in Old Town. Normally, somebody like Gareth wouldn't be running off to investigate this sort of thing. Miles had thought that more often, he would run away from trouble. But here they were, strolling through the twisting lanes of the worst part of Shanty Town. Both older men walked with hands on the hilts of daggers. Miles would have as well, were his not sheathed behind his back. He thought of just taking it out, but that sort of ostentation in this part of town was akin to asking for a fight.

Soon, the rickety wood shanties gave way to old ruined buildings. They were constructed of rough-cut stones piled together and held in place with mortar. Most of the mortar had decayed with time, and in some places the walls themselves were tumbling. The roofs must have all been timber because almost none of the buildings had one anymore. The stones were worn with age, chipped, and covered in moss and ivy. Here and there, vermin would skitter around the ruins. Sometimes, something larger lurked in the shadows.

There were people living here, and this was no secret to anybody. They were the most desperate, though, of all the people of Seahaven. Most of them were outlaws and fugitives. Pirates, murderers, rapists, and any other miscreant you could think of. If one had a high price on his head, Old Town was as good a place as any to hide. There were no businesses here and no homes, just the old, tumbled down ruins of what used to be the heart of the city. Wives' tales about ghosts and goblins and wild cannibals usually dissuaded anybody who might have thought of making a home in the ruins. Any reasonable person knew these stories were just fables, but few seemed to have the stones to test the theory. Regardless, there were so many criminals hiding out here that it wouldn't take ghosts or goblins to make it a dangerous place.

Now that they were in Old Town, all three of them became tense and wary. Filian had explained during the journey what they were looking for. He had said that people were being attacked, but this was nothing out of the ordinary in Old Town. What was unusual was the ferocity of the attacks. People also said dirt and ragged clothing covered the aggressors, and that they looked like they should be dead. This last piece of news seemed to have bothered Gareth. Miles wasn't sure why, but his mentor took on a much more serious tone after hearing this. He had told Miles to go back to his alley, or preferably the orphanage, but the intrepid young man had insisted on staying. Therefore, the three of them ended up here, hunting for the hunters in the shadows of the night.

A sudden scream pierced the silence of the night and alerted them their prey was nearby. Gareth took off at a sprint without hesitating, but Miles and Filian were close behind. They rounded the corner of one of the old, tumbled down ruins to find a woman backed against a wall. She was dressed as one would expect in this part of the city, in rough burlap and wool rags. Her face was full of terror, and her mouth open in a scream that had been silenced abruptly. Before her stood a man, or what might have been a man at one time. The creature's face was gaunt and shallow, its skin stretched too tight and split in places. The mouth of the thing hung open and cocked at an odd angle. Sticky drool formed webs between its rotten teeth, and an almost inaudible moan escaped the ragged throat. One hand clutched the woman's neck, choking the life out of her. The other hung limply. It wore the clothing of a merchant sailor, although the style was unfamiliar.

Gareth charged, drawing that strange obsidian sword from behind his back. Miles stood, shocked still from terror, and watched it all unfold. His mentor slashed at the decrepit thing, slicing easily through the arm holding the woman and severing the limb at the elbow. As the blade passed through its arm, the decrepit figure lurched back, but the hand choking the woman remained—and its grip did not lax. The creature turned to Gareth and opened its jaw in a what might have been a howl of rage had its throat not rotted away some long years ago. Instead, only a pitiful whine escaped its lips. It rushed at Gareth, trying to reach out with that limp arm but only swung it in a pendulous manner. Filian charged in at this point with a long, curved knife in each hand. He slashed at the thing over and over, but it did not seem phased. Miles saw no blood from the wounds. Onward it came at Gareth, desperately swinging that limp arm. He cut at it again and again, severing the arm and a leg. Now prone, the desiccated thing continued to crawl towards him. Still, the severed hand grasped at the woman's throat and her face was turning blue. Filian must have seen this, for he leaped to the maid's side and struggled to pry the fingers from her neck. Gareth sliced down at the thing on the ground, severing its head from its body. Still, it writhed, and the fingers of the severed arm on the ground continued to wriggle. Gareth chopped at it over and over, grunting in exertion. Finally, it was still.

Filian tore the last of the fingers from the woman's throat, breaking them off at the knuckles in places. She fell to the ground, sobbing and gasping for air. He held her, trying to offer some comfort. Gareth stood over the body of the creature he had killed, winded and panting. The obsidian sword hung limply from his hand. He stared at the thing, and Miles hesitantly crept up to his mentor's side. "What is it?" he asked.

Gareth simply shook his head, taking a few more deep breaths. "I have no idea."

Filian looked up from the woman and said, "Gareth, I know you've gotten yourself into some strange situations lately. You always try to keep me out of it. Did I get you into another one this time?" He was shaking, and Miles wasn't sure if he was comforting the sobbing woman, or she him.

"I think you did, friend," Gareth said.

"What now?" Miles asked.

"We need to find out what this thing is," Gareth said. He stood there for a moment longer, still staring down at the body that he had hacked to pieces. The skin was dry and tight, and no blood issued forth from any part of it. Drool still seemed to ooze from the mouth, but there was something unnatural about it. Worms and maggots wriggled out of the wounds and from the ears and nose of the thing. Miles turned and retched, falling to his knees. The woman's sobbing became frantic again.

"We need to go see Hector," Gareth said, turning to walk away without another word.

Miles and Filian looked at each other, both puzzled. "Who is Hector?" they both asked in unison.

Chapter Four

Miles stood in front of one of the walled estates in the Noble Quarter, wondering why fate had brought him to such a place. Gareth had led them there, to be sure. Still, the superstitious youth felt like this ominous night was being crafted by the hands of Shayla, goddess of fate. It was said that she wove the tapestry of life, and that each person was a thread in that tapestry. Shayla might twist the thread, passing it over others in places where two people are destined to meet. She might also cut a thread short, something Miles was worried about happening to his own thread at the moment. He could almost feel her pulling at him, tugging him ever onward on a path he would rather not take. He looked up at Gareth, who strode purposefully towards the iron gate which barred entrance to the manor beyond. Filian followed close behind, his own apprehension apparent.

A guard stood on either side of the gate. Each wore a steel breastplate over a padded red gambeson, and crested helmets topped their heads. They both held a short spear and had daggers at their belts. Altogether ordinary for either a city guard or a private one, and these two were surely the latter. One of them, a man with a thin, handlebar mustache, stepped towards the three of them with his spear held across his chest. "Stay back, scum. I don't know what you're doing in the Noble Quarter, but you had best get back to Shanty Town where you belong." The other man stood near, his spear also at the ready.

Gareth smiled that charming smile that had wooed so many women in the harbor taverns. He held his hands out, showing that he was not looking for a fight. "Oh dear, was our coming not announced? Please, be a good lad and fetch your master for me."

The mustachioed guard looked to the other man, who seemed to be his junior. He shrugged, as if to say that he knew nothing of guests. Mustachio turned back to Gareth and said, "The master is not expecting guests, and especially not common louts like your-selves. Be gone, or we'll be forced to stick ya."

Filian, who always seemed to itch for a fight, let his hands drift to the two long knives hanging from his belt. Gareth seemed to anticipate this, because he di-rected a warning glance at his friend. Miles stood by, his own hand tight on the handle of the knife behind his back. Gareth continued to speak, "That just won't do at all. Do you know how angry Hector would be if he heard you ran through his dear friend Gareth?" This last, he said quite loudly.

"Don't raise your voice to me," Mustachio said. "I don't know whose attention you're trying to get with all that caterwauling, but nobody else is around to hear you."

Just then, there was a sound of somebody coughing softly from behind the gate, as if to draw attention de-liberately. The younger of the guards turned, then snapped to attention and gave a slight bow. "Master! Evening, sir."

"Please," Hector said with a thick accent, "allow my guests to pass. I apologize for not announcing their visit, it seems to have... slipped my mind." Miles could barely see the man in the shadows behind the wall. He was tall and gaunt with angular features. His skin was terribly pale, as if he had been ill. He wore fancy clothes of black velvet and white satin, complete with polished shoes and a long dinner jacket. Ruffles of lace covered his slender neck, framed his face, and puffed out from his jacket's sleeves.

"Apologies, milord," Mustachio said, blushing bright red. He gave a hurried bow, then opened the gate.

"My thanks, good sir," Gareth said with a grin. He tossed a copper coin to the guard as he passed, sauntering through the gate of the manor as if it were his own estate.

Hector bid them to follow him to the house itself, but remained silent as they walked. He led them through a large hall complete with two arcing staircases. Beyond this, through a door to the left, he took them to a small parlor and invited them to sit. The ornate chairs were crafted from some sort of dark wood and had padded seats and backs covered in red velvet. The carpet in the room, as well, was deep red. A small fire burned in a modest hearth, and above the mantle hung a magnificent bastard sword of some foreign design. The room was pristine, and the wealth it contained far outweighed anything Miles had ever dreamed of seeing.

Gareth made himself comfortable, throwing one leg over the side of his chair and pulling his pipe out.

As he prepared to light it, Hector spoke up, "You are an audacious man, Gareth Vann."

"I'm going to take that as a compliment," Gareth said with that sly grin.

"A what?" Filian asked.

Hector glared at the other man, the red irises of his eyes making his piercing gaze that much more terrible. "Your friend doesn't have the same love of the written word that you do, does he?"

"Filian," Gareth said, gesturing to the other man, "and Miles."

"A pleasure, to be sure," Hector said, though his tone did not match the sentiment. The pale man walked over to a chair in the corner, far from the fire and nestled in shadow. He sat, crossed one leg over the other, and met Gareth's eyes with a hard stare.

After several moments of uncomfortable silence, Gareth spoke up, "This is where you ask, '*Why are you here?*' And then I say, '*We need your help.*'"

"No," Hector said bluntly. He clapped his hands loudly and shouted, "Ramone!"

Even Gareth seemed taken aback, while Miles and Filian both almost jumped out of their seats. Moments later, a man in a simple black suit entered the room bearing a silver platter. On top of it was a crystal carafe and several glasses. Hector gestured to his guests, and the man made his way about the room, handing each a glass and filling it with wine. "Never let one say I am not a gracious host." Hector smiled, revealing sharp canine teeth that seemed to be far too long.

As Ramone made his way around the room, Miles noticed scars on his neck, as if someone had stabbed him repeatedly with a large sewing needle. Some seemed fresh, others healed over, but all of them were in pairs. He looked to Gareth, who nodded and smiled at the younger thief before he said, "Hector, you're not having a glass?"

"My constitution does not agree with the nectar of the vine, I'm sorry to say," Hector explained.

"Does Ramone have anything else he can pour for you? Surely, he must see to it you are not thirsty," Gareth said as he scratched at his own neck.

Hector's eyes narrowed, and his carefully crafted smile became a scowl. "He does his duty, as our arrangement demands. Something, surely, you know nothing about."

"Words like thorns of a rose, thus does he strike at me so," Gareth said, grasping a feigned wound at his chest.

"Ramone, leave us," Hector said flatly. Once the servant had left the room, he said, "Your insolence is not welcome, human. I suggest you explain why you are here so that I may have the opportunity to dismiss you."

Miles shot glances between Hector and Gareth. *Human?* He wondered just who this Hector was.

Gareth sat up straight, suddenly becoming serious. "There's trouble in Old Town, and I want to know what's going on."

Hector cocked one eyebrow in either interest or surprise, then said, "And what would I know about this... Old Town... as you say?"

"I don't know," Gareth said. "But what would you say about dead men walking around attacking people?"

Hectors eyes widened as he sat upright, suddenly very engaged. "Be sure of what you are saying, Gareth Vann, and tell me what you saw."

Gareth relayed the events of the encounter earlier that night, describing the abomination that they had fought in the ruins. As he spoke, Hector's attention remained rapt. The slender man nodded again and again, no longer surprised but no less interested. Miles was very unnerved by this. Anybody else hearing about dead men walking the streets of the city would either panic or dismiss the news as folly. This strange man, however, seemed to accept every word. Even more, he did not seem surprised by the details.

"You have a problem, Gareth." Hector looked at Filian and Miles. "You all do."

"Wait just a minute," Filian spoke up finally. "This is all getting far too strange for me. I thought they were some diseased pirates or something, but now you're accepting what Gareth said? You think they were dead men walking?"

"Yes," Hector said.

Filian shook his head. "Thanks, but no thanks. This is too much for me."

Miles stood up, outraged. "You brought us there, you tramp. You got us into this and now you're just leaving?"

Filian nodded. "And if you're smart, little man, you'll do the same." With that, the other man saw himself out of the manor.

The parlor was silent for a few moments, but Gareth broke the interlude. "All the better that he not get more involved. We don't need every sneak with half a wit knowing about this."

Miles looked at him, suddenly aware that Gareth knew more than he was letting on.

"That suits me well. What about the young one?" Hector asked, eying Miles hungrily. The young man suddenly felt terrified, even though he was not sure why.

"He is under my protection," Gareth said, his tone full of threat.

Hector smiled, holding his hands up to calm the grisly thief. "Please, friend, do not fret. I simply... enjoy the smell of the boy."

Miles looked to Gareth, his heart pounding in his chest. He heard the words passing between the two men, but he was sure that there was an undertone to the conversation that he wasn't privy to. Furthermore, he was sure that this secret dialog somehow involved him in a most intimate way.

Gareth frowned, not liking the direction that the conversation was taking. "Back to business, Hector. What do you know about this?"

"Specifically, nothing. In general?"

"Anything would be helpful."

"Very well. You are most likely dealing with a necromancer."

"A what?" Gareth said, for the first time since they arrived showing any sign of not being in control of the situation.

"One who dabbles in parting the veil between the world of the living, and the world of the dead. They often attempt to create servants out of what once was dead," Hector explained.

"Like you?" Gareth asked. At this, Hector hissed sharply.

Miles was so taken aback that he dropped his glass of wine on the floor. "What are you two talking about? The dead? Hector is dead?" Panic rose in his voice and he started looking around for an escape route by instinct.

Gareth walked over to the younger man, placing his hands on his shoulders. "Miles, this is me you're talking about. You know I wouldn't let anybody hurt you. You wanted to learn the shadow craft from me. I didn't want this to happen yet, but it's time for the next step in your education."

Miles looked over to Hector, who feigned a smile. "Back to what you were saying, Gareth. No, not like me. These creatures that the necromancer is making are abominations. It is so in the eyes of a human, or an immortal."

"A what?" Miles asked.

"Later," Gareth chided, then to Hector he said, "Whatever you say. Now, how do we find this... necromancer?"

"You will need the help of somebody who knows that part of the city better than myself," Hector said. "But I can tell you this: find a cemetery there, and you may find newly emptied graves. If you do, that is where you will stalk your prey."

Chapter Five

Miles and Gareth walked along the city streets. The predawn glow of the sky heralded the coming of the sun. Miles stretched and yawned, ready for this night to be over. Almost a day ago, he was stealing fish for breakfast. Since then he had scrubbed pots, herded children, broken into a home, met with the owner, walked to Old Town, watched Gareth kill a dead man, walked to the Noble Quarter, and talked to another dead man? Miles would have been sure that he was dreaming if he wasn't so tired.

"More than you were expecting, isn't it?" Gareth asked.

Miles stopped, setting his hands on his hips. "I expected to steal a few coins, a few fish, and a loaf of bread. I didn't expect to be fighting dead men — or talking to them."

Gareth stopped and turned, a pained look on his face. "I didn't want to get you involved in all of this, at least not yet. I had hoped that you could avoid it, but you and I are too much alike. As much as we want to run from trouble, we always end up walking right towards it for some reason."

"It's Shayla," Miles said.

Gareth laughed, but the look of scorn from Miles stopped his brevity. "The lady of fate, is it? Well, you ask Hector next time you see him, and he will tell you what he told me when we first met." With that, the older man turned and continued walking down the cobbled street.

Miles hesitated, then hurried to catch up and ask, "What did he tell you?"

Gareth turned and smiled, "We make our own luck."

Miles thought about that for a moment. He had always thought that the lady of fate was pulling at his thread, and at the threads of everybody else. He knew Gareth had not been one to talk much of the gods, but he was superstitious when it came to luck. To hear him say that he made his own luck was a new concept for the boy. "How can that be?"

"Well," Gareth said, "I told you to go back before we went to Old Town, right?"

Miles nodded.

"Had you done so, you would have had a quiet evening. Maybe you would have pilfered that loaf of bread and a few copper bits along the way, but in all, it would have been an uneventful night. Instead, you insisted on coming with Filian and I. So, all the strangeness that you have found yourself wrapped up in is of your own doing."

Miles opened his mouth to argue but couldn't find any words that made sense. He clapped shut his jaws and walked along next to Gareth sullenly. After a while, he realized they had walked through most of Shanty Town. The blacksmith shop, and even Gareth's own small cottage, were already far behind them. The dawn sky silhouetted the masts of ships, and he knew they were close to the harbor. "Where are we going?"

"To see a friend," Gareth replied.

"What about sleep?"

"There will be time later. For now, we need to talk to somebody."

"I hope he's not as creepy as your other friend," Miles said, suddenly not wanting to meet anybody else that Gareth knew.

Gareth chuckled at this but said no more. Soon, they were standing in front of a rough and run-down, two-story building. The wood planks showed signs of having been many assorted colors in the past, but were mostly bare wood now. The walls were cobbled together piecemeal, and most of the boards looked like they were taken from the deck of a ship and reused here. The place smelled of the most wretched of humanity. Vomit, piss, alcohol, and worse all mingled in the air. The place was quiet at this hour. A few patrons were sleeping off their night of revelry on the building's front porch. An obscene depiction of two fish mating was painted on the sign above the door. Gareth gestured towards the door and said, "Welcome to the Two Fishes, the most disreputable inn Seahaven has to offer."

Miles wrinkled his nose as he looked up at the sign. "I thought The Lusty Mermaid was bad."

Grinning, Gareth said, "Why do you think I never brought you here before?"

The inside of the inn was no better than the exterior, including the presence of several snoring bodies strewn about the place. The bar was untended, but there was a large dog gnawing on a bone behind it. Miles looked over at the beast, which growled menacingly.

"I wouldn't bother old Mabel," Gareth said.

"She seems nice enough," Miles joked.

"Yeah, until she tears your arm off at the elbow. She keeps the bottles where they belong while Fergus sleeps."

Miles reluctantly followed him up the narrow, crooked stairs. The way was dark and unlit, and Miles was sure that he had touched several types of bodily fluids on the wall as he struggled to keep his balance. The hall upstairs was lit only by a few candles, and no less dim than the stairs. At the end of the hall they came to an unassuming door that looked no different from any other, save that this one actually had a lock set into it. Gareth raised his fist and banged loudly on the door several times. He waited, listening for movement inside, then knocked again.

"A moment, a moment, if you will!" came the irritated response from inside. "Who comes calling at this blasted hour?"

"A friend," Gareth said.

"Indeed?"

Gareth frowned at the reply, for some reason seeming very irritated. "Open the door, old man. There's trouble."

There was a rustling from inside the door, then the sound of a chain being unfastened and moved aside. Then another, and another. Finally, the lock clicked, and the door cracked open. Through the crack, Miles saw a man who was a bit older than Gareth. He had a pointed beard and a thin mustache, both with more than a touch of gray to them. His hair was receding, and the color at the temples matched his beard. He squinted at both Gareth and Miles in turn, as if struggling to see. "By the stars, Gareth. It's been some time." With that, the older man opened the door and invited the two of them inside.

"Nikolai," Gareth said to the man, "this is Miles."

The man, this Nikolai, squinted at Miles and then smiled. He extended his hand in welcome, which the boy cautiously shook. He was relieved, at least, that this man didn't seem to be dead.

"A son?" Nikolai asked. "You never mentioned the boy."

Gareth shook his head. "No, a friend. More like a student, really."

"Indeed," Nikolai said.

Gareth winced. "Yes, *indeed*. I've been teaching him the shadow craft, but last night his training advanced to a field that is more of your expertise." With that, they sat and discussed the events of the night before. Gareth described the dead man that had tried to strangle the woman. He told of the brief battle, and how he had to hack the thing to pieces before it would stop moving. He did not, however, mention the visit with Hector.

"What about..." Miles started, but Gareth cut him off.

"And that's all we know," Gareth said, glaring at Miles. For some reason, the older man did not want Nikolai to know about Hector. It seemed to Miles that his old friend had a lot of secrets these days, and not just from his young apprentice.

Nikolai paced the room, tugging at his beard. He had been quiet thus far, and seemed to contemplate the situation. "It seems," he said finally, "that we have a necromancer on our hands."

Miles shot a glance to Gareth, whose returned glare was enough to keep him quiet.

Gareth stood and walked over to where Nikolai stood staring out of the window. "Tell me, what do you know of these necromancers?"

"They toy with the life energies that bind us to this world. The concept is... difficult to comprehend." Nikolai hesitated, seemingly struggling to explain. "Each of us has a certain spark of life, if you will. The necromancer seeks to manipulate that spark. Some have found ways to snuff it out. Others, ways to reignite it after death. Some, of the more sinister sort, create an artificial spark inside something that should be dead."

"The thing I fought," Gareth said.

"Indeed, it seems that is likely. They are called ghouls by those who study them. Bodies of the dead given a second chance to walk among the living. The results, though, are usually malicious. Only the basest instincts exist in the animated dead. To protect themselves, and to feed. Beyond this, they are mindless."

"Why would anybody make these things?" Miles spoke up.

Nikolai smiled at the boy, then said to Gareth, "He is curious, just like you are. You choose well, it seems."

Gareth harrumphed, then winked at Miles.

"Well," Nikolai continued, "some experiment with these dark sciences, or magics if one will indulge the fancy, purely for the sake of knowledge. Others, however, find some use for these ghouls. One can give them simple tasks to perform, if they are kept fed. Otherwise, they seek only to kill and dine on the flesh of the living."

"How could that body have held together, though?" Gareth asked. "It must have been a hundred years old or more."

Nikolai thought on this for a moment, again tugging at his beard. "The salt," he said.

Gareth and Miles both waited for further explanation, which was not forthcoming. Finally, Nikolai seemed to realize they were waiting for him to say more. "The ground beneath the cliffs is rich in salt from the sea. In fact, the entire city sits atop salted soil. The bodies buried by the first settlers here were set to rest directly in the soil, which has preserved their flesh and kept them from rotting away. Some centuries-old cemetery is the ideal place to find subjects for such experimentation." Nikolai seemed excited by the prospect.

"Nikolai," Gareth cautioned, "don't get any ideas."

"What? Oh. No, of course not. The genius of it all is simply thrilling to consider. To think, what type of man has concluded to use these preserved corpses for his tasks?"

"A twisted one, I would say," Miles suggested.

"He is definitely a lot like you," Nikolai said to Gareth.

Gareth simply ignored this and said, "So, we need to find a cemetery in Old Town?"

Nikolai seemed far away. "What? Oh. Indeed, I suppose that would do. Then mayhap you can catch the necromancer as he procures his next specimen."

"How are we going to find some forgotten grave-yard in Old Town?" Miles asked, yawning.

"You need a guide," Nikolai said. "But given the usual denizens of that part of the city, you will need to enlist someone of the most unsavory sort."

Gareth smiled. "I know just the man for the job."

Chapter Six

The two thieves stood before another nondescript door in the Two Fishes Inn, this one on the main floor. They had sneaked past Mabel the dog, through the filthy kitchen, and finally to this simple door near the back of the building. Loud snoring issued forth from inside, sounding almost like the growl of a dragon. Miles looked at Gareth apprehensively, knowing what sort of beast lie within this lair.

"You can't be serious," Miles said.

Gareth cocked an eyebrow at him. "And you have a better idea?"

Miles shook his head.

The older man knocked on the door, but the snoring from inside didn't even change its rhythm. He turned the simple knob and cracked the door open, squeaking on rusty hinges. The creaking grew louder as Gareth opened it, yet whatever rested inside was undisturbed. "Water," he said.

Miles ran out back, filling a bucket with rainwater from a barrel. He brought it to Gareth, who took the bucket in both hands and doused the bed inside the chamber with the liquid.

The man in the bed spat out a mouthful of water, sat up straight as a plank, and yelled, "Close those hatches, you worthless sea dogs! See to the yard arm and furl the sails. There be a storm coming!"

Gareth laughed as the man floundered about in his bed, struggling to determine if he was drowning at sea or not. Miles looked on in astonishment, wondering if this would be the last day he spent with his mentor. The man he had just awoken was known for his temper. He also had a reputation for crushing men's skulls with one hand. Fergus, the owner of the Two Fishes, was a giant of a man. Sitting in the bed, he was as tall as Gareth was standing. Once on his feet, he would stand a head and shoulder taller. His own shoulders were as broad as two men or more, and his arms were like tree branches bulging with cannonballs for muscles. His broad, bronze chest was covered in curly black hair, and he had a dark beard trimmed into a perfect square. His head was shaved and a blue tattoo of an octopus covered most of it, with tentacles worming their way down his neck. There were other tattoos, as well. Ships, anchors, sails, stars, and busty women adorned his arms and belly. From one ear hung a large loop of gold, but otherwise the giant was completely undressed. Miles was shocked to find, in fact, that the man was anatomically proportionate no matter where the eye wandered.

Gareth threw a jerkin and some pants that were lying on the floor at the big man and said, "Cover that thing up, Fergus, before you scare the boy."

Fergus grunted, trying to hide a smile at the jest. He put on the sternest face he could muster and said, "Gareth Vann, you had better have a really good reason to be waking me up like that. If not, you better not have any regrets to take with you to the next life."

"I think I'm going to go with the first option," Gareth said, no longer smiling.

Fergus seemed to realize the seriousness of his tone and hurriedly dressed himself. "What is it?"

Gareth explained briefly what Nikolai had told them, again failing to mention anything about Hector. Miles picked up on this, but kept any questions he might have about it to himself, for now.

"You're bloody kidding me," Fergus said.

"I wish it were so, old friend," Gareth replied.

"Now, I've seen some crazy things in my time. Out on the sea, I'll tell you, stuff happens out there that you couldn't imagine. This, though? This is just downright perverse," the big man said.

"So, you'll help us?" Miles asked.

Fergus smiled down at the younger man, who barely came up to his biceps. He laid a gentle hand on the boy's shoulder and said, "Yes, young master thief, I will help you."

*   *   *

Miles and Gareth took some time to rest that morning, while Fergus gathered some supplies and arranged for somebody to tend the inn for him in his absence. Usually the big man didn't like anybody else tending his bar. He didn't trust anybody, and for good reason.

Maybe it was the old pirate in him, but he knew people were dishonest by nature. He called in a favor from Jacob, the owner of The Lusty Mermaid. Soon the Maid's premier serving girl, Marcella, was standing behind the bar of the Two Fishes. She brought along two of her cousins, both rather large men, to fill the role of bouncer. That, also, Fergus usually took care of himself.

After a few hours of sleep, Gareth and Miles trudged into the taproom. Fergus was preparing some food for them, and Marcella came over to the table with two mugs of steaming coffee. "Why is it that whenever trouble is brewing in this city, Gareth Vann is at the heart of it?" she asked with a playful smile.

"Lucky, I guess," Gareth said as he yawned and tried to work the tightness from his joints.

"I thought you said that you make your own luck?" Miles quipped.

Marcella cocked an eyebrow at this. "Oh, is that so? The same way Filian does with his dice?"

Gareth chuckled. "No, not quite like that."

"Well, you boys try not to get into too much trouble. I'm sure Fergus can handle just about anything, but I'd still rather see you back in one piece." With that, she planted a warm kiss on Gareth's cheek and sauntered away. Both he and Miles almost fell out of their chairs as they leaned over to watch her departure.

"What are you looking at?" Gareth asked the boy.

"Same thing as you, old man," Miles replied, smiling as he took a sip of coffee.

Fergus entered the taproom from the kitchen, a tray of steaming plates in his large hands. He set down an assortment of salted pork, smoked fish, and boiled eggs. Nothing fancy, but for the two men who had been out all night dealing with the walking dead, it was satisfying. By the time they left the Two Fishes, the sun was creeping up in the sky. It was almost noon, and the summer heat was oppressive. Sweat broke out on all three men within minutes of beginning their journey. Fortunately for them, they didn't have far to go. Old Town, being nestled under the cliffs that supported Castle Ravencrest, was close to the harbor.

"So, you were a pirate?" Miles asked, hoping to pass the time. He also wanted to distract himself from thoughts of the night before and what was to come.

"Aye, I was," Fergus said.

"Miles, maybe you should ask me before you go digging up somebody's past?" Gareth admonished.

Fergus held out a hand. "No, it's all right. Everybody knows my story." He looked at Miles and grinned. "Well, almost everybody."

"Why did you buy an inn?" Miles asked.

"Here we go," Gareth muttered under his breath.

"Well," Fergus started, "that's a long story. I was in the crew of a man called Jacobson. His ship, the Bloody Wench, was the terror of the Eastern Sea."

Gareth cleared his throat loudly. "Fergus, that is a long story. Maybe another time?"

Fergus frowned. "Fine, then. I won't spoil it for you, young Miles. We'll just have to wait for another time to tell that tale. Trust me, though, it's a good one."

Miles nodded, then asked, "So, you spent time in Old Town after that?"

"Aye, I did at that. Before, during, after. I've spent a lot of time in those old ruins, hiding or running. Everybody there is either hiding or running from something."

"Which is why Fergus is helping us," Gareth said. The big man nodded.

"Why?" Miles asked.

Gareth explained, "Fergus still knows some people here. Some good, some bad..."

"Mostly bad," Fergus interrupted.

"Regardless, he knows it's a rough life, but walking corpses trying to eat people is worse than anybody here deserves," Gareth finished.

"Why are we dealing with this, and not the city guard?" Miles asked.

Gareth and Fergus both laughed at this, then the old pirate took over the explaining. "They don't care, laddie. Unless some fat cat is losing coin, there's no reason for the city guard to get involved. Somebody makes some corpses everybody forgot about start walking, and they kill some criminals nobody cares about? Why get involved?"

Miles frowned. He knew the city guard was always going to be a rival of his, as a thief. He had thought, though, that they at least worked to keep the people safe. He had respected them for that. This spin on things made him reconsider that. "What about protecting the people?"

Gareth added, "They protect rich people and their coin, nothing more. The people of Shanty Town could start tearing each other apart, and the only reason they might get involved is to keep the workforce from being reduced overly much."

"Is this a class on politics, or are we going to kill a necromancer?" Fergus asked, the last word still feeling strange on his tongue.

"Right you are," Gareth said. "So, where's this cemetery?"

"Not far," Fergus said as they wove their way through the crumbling ruins of Old Town. There had been a good amount of traffic in the streets of the Harbor District at this time of day, but now there was not a soul to be seen. If this part of the city seemed near deserted at night, it was like a ghost town during the day.

Finally, they found it. There was a low wall surrounding the cemetery, topped with an iron fence. The iron was rusted, and a good half of the bars were missing or broken. The wall itself was made of the same roughhewn stone and mortar as the surrounding buildings. That, too, was crumbling from disrepair. The entire graveyard itself was only a few hundred feet across in either direction and littered with a hodgepodge of distinctive style headstones. Many of these were cracked and broken. There was a simple mausoleum near the back of the yard, presumably the resting place of the first lords of Seahaven. Behind this, the stone cliff that held up Castle Ravencrest rose towards the sky for almost three hundred feet.

"Here we are, now what?" Fergus asked.

Gareth was looking around, not at the cemetery, but at the nearby buildings. Miles walked among the headstones, trying to decipher engravings worn by centuries of salty sea air. Gareth had started teaching him to read, and this would have been a good time to test his skills. Those words that were still somewhat legible, however, were in strange languages. It was said that the first settlers in Seahaven had come from many distant lands, and the variety of characters carved into the ancient stones was a testament to this. There were a few graves, Miles noticed, that had been recently dug and refilled. Since nobody had been laid to rest here for hundreds of years, Miles assumed someone had robbed these graves of their occupants.

"Over here," Gareth called out, waving at the others from a building across the street. It was larger than most and had at one time likely stood three stories tall. The stones were larger, too, especially the massive cornerstones. "Probably an old temple," Gareth said.

"I always thought so," Fergus added, "given it's so close to the graveyard."

Miles looked up at the tumbling edifice, wondering what ancient gods were worshiped here in the past. The ground floor was mostly whole, but the ceiling which would have also served as the floor of the next level had long ago rotted away. There was evidence of wood beams in the form of square holes carved into the stone at regular intervals. The walls, as they rose higher, became more and more damaged. The only evidence of a third floor was a single spire of stone that looked like a crooked finger pointing to the Duke's castle. In all, the old temple looked like a gnarled hand, cursing the ancient keep above for letting its peers crumble into ruin.

"This will be a good place to hide and wait," Gareth said, climbing into the building over a pile of rubble. The others followed him, picking their way through the loose stone carefully. Fergus had to bend low to crawl through the opening in the wall, his shoulders scraping the stones above.

"I'm not used to hiding," Fergus muttered.

"You'll do fine," Miles said. "Just try to be small."

Fergus shot him a glare that could have bored a hole in the side of a ship, and Gareth stifled a hearty laugh.

Chapter Seven

It was a long wait for nightfall, and they passed the time telling tales of adventures long in the past. Gareth had some wild tales from his own youth, usually involving either coin or women. Fergus shared some amazing stories from his time as a pirate on the Bloody Wench, including how the ship got its name. The first captain of the ship had been a woman, one Mary Hatcher. She had a notorious reputation for violence, so people took to calling her Bloody Mary. The name stuck, and she took full advantage of the moniker to inspire fear in her potential victims and rivals alike. She even went so far as to have the figurehead of the ship, a beautiful carving of a busty maiden, painted over with splatters and runs of red. She renamed the ship to match the new ghastly figurehead and rechristened her as the Bloody Wench.

"What was it called before?" Miles asked.

"Oh, I don't know. That was before I joined up with Captain Jacobson," Fergus said.

"Shh!" Gareth shushed them and gestured out past the opening in the crumbling temple wall. There, in the cemetery across the street, was the bobbing light of a lantern. It cast two cadaverous shadows behind it, dancing along the cliff face like twisted marionettes.

Miles crept up to the wall and looked out, squinting to focus in the darkness. The lantern was set down, and he could see two men standing there. They both wore long brown coats pulled tight about them, and tricorne hats topped their heads. One man had a bushy beard, and the other mutton chops. They both appeared to have seen less than thirty summers, but were weathered as if they had led hard lives. They had shovels in hand and seemed to be deciding on a place to dig.

"Is one of them the necromancer?" Miles whispered.

Gareth shook his head. "I don't know."

Fergus was looming over the two of them, trying to stay low in the shadows. "Well, I guess we just kill them both?"

"No," Gareth said. "If neither of them is the necromancer, then they're both working for him. We need them alive to tell us how to find him."

Fergus frowned. The big man loved a good fight, but not getting to crush your opponent's skull in the end was anticlimactic.

"Let us get the drop on them," Gareth said. "Then, you do what you do best, but without the killing."

"Fine," Fergus grumbled.

Gareth crept out of their hiding spot, motioning for Miles to follow. Silently, they moved around to one end of the cemetery where the shadows of the cliff above blocked out the moonlight. They moved swiftly between the headstones; their quarry unaware. Gareth had a dagger in each hand, blades turned down and pommels extending past his closed fists. Miles had picked up a shaft of rusty iron from the crumbling walls, holding it before him like a staff. The older man struck first, leaping from the shadows like a pouncing cat. He struck the bearded man below the base of his skull with one of the dagger's pommels. The man cried out in shock and pain, then crumpled to the ground. Miles charged at the man with the mutton chops, swinging his iron bar clumsily. His attack was parried with a shovel, and soon the two were engaged in a deadly dance of stick fighting with their improvised weapons.

Gareth circled around the man while Fergus charged across the street, bellowing like some jungle heathen. Again and again, Miles matched his opponent blow for blow. The iron bar clanged against the wood handle of the shovel, and his hands ached from the reverberations. His mentor tried landing blows from the flank, but the wild swings of the shovel kept him from getting close enough. Finally, Fergus entered the fray and crashed into the smaller man with a grunt. They both tumbled to the ground, rolling over each other in a flurry of limbs and shouts. The shovel went flying, nearly missing Miles' head.

"Stop wiggling, dammit!" Fergus shouted as he slammed his ham-sized fist into the man's face again and again. Gareth sheathed his daggers and grabbed his old friend from behind, struggling to drag him away.

"Enough!" Gareth shouted.

Miles looked at the man on the ground in horror. His nose was surely broken, and blood gurgled out from it and his mouth. Teeth slid down his cheeks in the deluge. The man was alive, though, as evidenced by the bubbles of air in the blood and his weak moaning. Nearby, Gareth held Fergus back, trying to calm him from his blind rage. The big man had a reputation for a short temper and fits of violence, but Miles had never seen a man beaten the way Fergus had pummeled the misshapen figure now sprawled before him.

In the chaos, he almost missed the other man running into the shadows. Busy controlling the giant of a man, Gareth had not seen the digger recover from his blow. Miles saw him, though, and quickly gave chase. Still clutching the iron bar in his hand, Miles ran through the cemetery, weaving between headstones. The other man scrambled over the broken wall, allowing Miles to catch up as he gracefully leaped over the debris. The shadows of the cliff cast darkness over this part of Old Town, but Miles could still hear the heavy footfalls ahead of him. He ducked around the corner of a ruined house and followed the sound to the right. The man was staying close to the cliffs, keeping to the darkness. This was something Miles would have done himself. Fortunately for him, the man wore heavy-soled boots and was making a lot of noise.

Deftly, Miles vaulted over low, crumbling walls and darted between broken stones. He avoided having to navigate the twisting streets by using the acrobatics that Gareth had been teaching him to pass through the ruined buildings. He lifted himself through windows and rolled on the ground on the other side. Always, he came out of the roll into a leap and landed on his feet. The footfalls were still far ahead of him, but he was sure that he was gaining ground. Eventually the man would run out of shadow, forcing him to come out into the moonlight.

The air burned in his lungs as Miles continued to run after the man. Where was he going? Most likely, the man was just running headlong through the shadows in hopes of escape. It was possible, however, that he was returning to some sort of hideout. If he was lucky, Miles might find out where the necromancer was operating from. We make our own luck, Gareth had said the night before. Miles gritted his teeth as he pumped his legs even harder. His vision seemed to focus in on every obstacle before him. The pulse pounding in his ears slowed as he ran. Soon, all he could hear was those heavy boots pounding on cracked stone street ahead of him. Sweat dripped from his brow in the warm night air, and his blond locks were plastered to his scalp.

He wasn't sure why he was trying to catch this man so badly. He hadn't wanted to get involved in this mess with necromancers and ghouls. He still had to ask Gareth what a vampire was, what Hector was. It seemed that there were many more secrets in the shadows of Seahaven than he had suspected. *I guess I am like him*, he thought, *always walking into trouble instead of running away from it*. He knew people who lived near here. There were kindly people on the streets of Shanty Town that waved and said hello to him. There was Nathan, Liam, and Hatha. The thought of one of those shambling creatures tearing the flesh of the young girl made him shudder as he ran. That was why he was chasing the man. He cared about the people he knew, and he didn't want to see them get hurt. They wouldn't get hurt if he could do something about it.

Still, he was terrified. He was accustomed to running away from people, not chasing them. He knew his heart was pounding as much from fear as it was from the physical exertion. What would he even do when he caught the man? He and Gareth had barely held off the other man until Fergus tackled him. How would he subdue the man with a rusty iron bar? He looked down for a moment and realized that blood was running down his hands where the jagged metal had sliced into his flesh. But he was so focused, he didn't feel any pain.

Suddenly, the footfalls stopped ahead of Miles. Slowing his own pace, he crept up to the corner of a small shack. He hadn't even realized that they had left Old Town behind and were now in one of the Shanty Town slums. How far had he run? He wasn't sure. Creeping around the building, he saw the man in the tricorne hat and long coat walking up to another shanty. This one was leaning against a hill which would slope up to join the cliffs behind them. The man looked over his shoulder. Miles ducked down, pressing himself as close as he could to the wood planks of the shack. The man didn't see him, though, because he entered the other shanty. Miles walked over, looking around cautiously. Was the man hiding in there, ready with a knife? Or worse, a crossbow?

The young thief approached from the side of the door and listened. He heard no movement inside, so he cracked the door open slightly. There was a single candle burning on a table inside, but he saw no occupant other than some other sparse furniture. *Where did he go?* Miles entered the shanty and poked around with a careful eye for detail. Nothing was out of place except for the rug. In a hovel like this, a floor lined with straw would be the norm. A woven sisal mat might have been a luxury here, yet there was a wool rug on the floor; green with yellow knot-work patterns embroidered into it. "This doesn't belong here," Miles whispered. He took out his dirk and slid the blade under the rug, carefully lifting it from the edge. As he lifted it higher, he saw a trap door underneath. "Got you."

Chapter Eight

Miles walked through the night on unsteady legs. His pulse still pounded in his ears as he dragged one leg in front of the other. He had exhausted himself in the chase, but he wasn't done yet. Having found the trapdoor, he faced a hard decision. Continue the chase to whatever lie below, or return to the others and tell them what he found. Considering that he wasn't sure what to do when he caught the man in the tricorne hat, he also wasn't sure what to do if he went through that hidden door. The man he had chased could be the necromancer, or he could just be a crony hired to dig up graves. If that were the case, he would have two men to deal with. Worse than that, there could be more of the ghouls down there. Alone, there was nothing that Miles could accomplish by continuing the chase.

So, he walked back into Old Town. He was alone and in no condition for a fight, but he was too tired to be afraid. This was the most direct way to get back to Gareth and Fergus. He still wasn't sure how long it had been since they parted, but he could only hope that they would still be there. As he passed the tumbledown, ancient ruins, he let the metal bar slip from his hands. It clanged to the street with an awful racket, shattering the silence of the night. He knew that there could be murderous pirates hiding in the shadows, but he trudged down the center of the street. Several times, he stumbled on cracked stones. He fell a few times, but always picked himself up.

He reached the cemetery and the old temple after what seemed like ages of walking. "Gareth?" he called out, but received no reply. The graveyard was empty, and the only signs of the struggle were two abandoned shovels and a pile of drying blood and sticky teeth. He checked the temple, but there as well he found no sign of his friend. "Fergus?" he cried. Again, the night was silent. Miles kept walking past the cemetery. He passed by the low stone buildings without even a glance down the side alleys. He made his way between wooden shacks and soon could smell the salty, fishy scent of the harbor.

It was nearly dawn again by the time Miles staggered through the door of the Two Fishes. Sweat soaked through his shirt, and his hair clung limply to his head. Gareth and Marcella both ran over to him, helping him to the nearest chair. Fergus was there, behind the bar, and even Nikolai had left his private room. It seemed they were all waiting for him, or maybe mourning his passage.

Gareth was the first to speak. "Miles, where did you go?"

Miles breathed a few ragged breaths, then rasped, "I found him." After that, he slumped over into oblivion.

*　　*　　*

When he opened his eyes, bright light stung them. He squeezed them closed, groaning with pain running all over his body.

75

"He's awake," somebody said.

"Fetch some water," a woman demanded.

He opened his eyes again, and this time the sting wasn't so bad. The sun glared in through a window, and he was lying on a soft bed—softer than anything he had ever laid on before. He looked around the room, blinking the blurriness from his eyes. There were books strewn about. Gareth was there, sitting in a chair by the bed and smoking his pipe. Nikolai and Marcella were there, too. Fergus came barging through the door, holding a clay pitcher that looked like a drinking glass in his massive hands. Marcella took it and poured water into a cup, handing it to Miles.

He drank it all in one breath and held it out for more before he had the air to speak. Soon, he had gone through half the pitcher and felt too full to continue, but still thirsty. "How long?" he asked.

"Almost all day. The sun is just now about to set," Gareth said.

"You had us worried, young'un," Fergus added.

"Indeed," Nikolai remarked.

Gareth shot a glance at the scholar, then turned back to Miles. "You said you found him before you passed out. You found the necromancer?"

"I think so," Miles said as he struggled to sit upright. He now realized that he was in Nikolai's room in the Two Fishes. "I followed the other man. I really don't know how far or for how long, but he went into a shack with a hidden door under a rug."

"Great," Gareth huffed.

"What is it?" Marcella asked as she tended to Miles. She leaned over him, wiping his brow with a wet cloth. Her ample bosom jiggled right in front of his face, close enough to smell her sweat. *Maybe this hero thing isn't all bad?* he thought.

"Probably some sort of cave or something. Who knows what's down there," Gareth explained.

Fergus nodded. "Most likely some old smuggler's tunnel. Might lead to a cave on the shore or in the cliffs. It could go for miles."

"I guess we'll have to go down there and try to find him," Gareth said, not happy at the prospect.

"Sounds like you're going to need help," a voice said from the hall outside of the room.

Everybody tensed at the intrusion. Gareth sprung to his feet, drawing a dagger. Fergus, already by the door, prepared to pounce on whoever was eavesdropping on them. The big innkeeper looked out into the hallway with a raised fist, but relaxed once he saw who was there.

"You son of a bitch! I almost smashed ya," Fergus said.

Miles leaned over in the bed, looking around Gareth. Filian walked into the room, hands held wide and with a roguish grin. "Hi," he said.

"What are you doing here, Filian?" Gareth asked as he sheathed his dagger.

"Hi, Filian. Nice to see you too, Filian," Filian mocked.

"Can I smash him, anyway?" Fergus asked, but Marcella's cutting look was all the answer he needed.

Filian gave Fergus a squint-eyed glare of his own, but there was more jest than threat to it. "We thought you could use some help."

"Filian, I thought you decided it was best to stay away from this," Gareth said, then hesitated. "Wait, did you say *we*?"

"Come downstairs," Filian said, then headed down the hall without waiting for any reply. He led them downstairs, and there in the taproom stood a dozen men. They were a motley mob, and that would be putting things kindly. The men were an assortment of rogues and pirates, grizzled veterans to the last man.

They held an assortment of weapons in their hands, ranging from a belaying pin to a bardiche.

"Oy, what's this?" Fergus asked as he came down the stairs. Gareth and the others were right behind him. Even Miles had dragged himself to his feet.

"Well, last night I had a few drinks at the Maid. One thing led to another, and I started spouting off at the mouth about that thing we fought in Old Town," Filian said.

"And we 'ere thought, this ain' right, it's not," a bald man with a long, braided beard spoke up from the gathering. He had two short axes hanging from his belt. Those around him nodded and grunted in agreement.

Filian nodded. "Like he said, whatever he said."

"Well," Gareth sighed, "seems like we've got ourselves a mob. Now we just have to go put them to work."

"How did you find us?" Miles asked.

"Oh," Filian said with a grin, "Jacob mentioned Marcella was helping out here, so I figured Gareth must have asked Fergus for help."

"I still want to smash him," Fergus grumbled under his breath.

Just then, a man burst through the front door. His face was panic-stricken he was covered in blood. "Fergus!"

"Brock?" Fergus asked as he approached the man. "What is it?"

The man, a sailor from the look of him, was shaking as he answered, "There's some sort of attack. There's people being chased through the streets and... eaten."

Fergus looked to Gareth, who said, "Ghouls. It's too late to come up with fancy plans."

"What do we do?" Miles asked.

Gareth thought for a moment, scratching the stubble on his cheek. He looked around at the assembled men, then said, "Miles, you come with me. We're going after the man responsible for this. The rest of you, go kill anything that looks like it should already be dead."

Fergus beamed and walked behind the bar. Reaching under, he came back up with a huge wood mallet in his hands. The handle of the weapon was as long as Miles was tall, and the head of it had to weigh ten pounds or more. Fergus easily hefted it over one shoulder and said, "Finally, let's go have some fun, boys!"

Chapter Nine

The sun was settling behind Baron's Hill by the time Brock brought the news of the attacks. The day was fading, and darkness encroached. Miles could hear screaming outside now. He couldn't believe this was happening. He had seen the ghoul, and chased the man who was digging up graves, but the thought of those creatures stalking the streets en mass was too terrifying to comprehend. He sat heavily in a chair, looking down at his bandage-wrapped hands. Blood still seeped through where the rusted bar had cut him. He bled for the city. And now, he and Gareth were going to go hunt down the necromancer alone? Miles couldn't figure out how he had gone from an average thief to a monster hunter in two days.

Marcella was sobbing nearby, and Nikolai tried to comfort her. "Come, miss. Let us leave the butcher's work to the young boys. You and I should go upstairs and have a drink to calm the nerves."

Gareth looked to the older man with fire in his eyes. "You will take care of her?"

"Indeed. No matter what may come," Nikolai answered. He then led Marcella up the stairs.

Fergus bellowed, "A'right, boys. Let's go get 'em." With that, he led the mob of miscreants out of the Two Fishes. Filian was by his side, his two long knives in hand. Behind them the others cheered and shouted, eager to do their bloody work.

Miles looked on in puzzlement while Gareth walked to the corner of the room and picked up a broom. He studied it as if evaluating a piece of art, but it was just an ordinary straw broom with a wood handle. He walked over to the bar, grasped the handle in two hands, and swung with all his might. It struck the bar with a resounding crack, and the end of it broke off. Gareth smiled, then walked over and handed the broken handle to Miles. He took the shaft of wood, looking up at his mentor with questioning eyes.

"You handled that iron bar fairly well, but this ought to serve you better," Gareth said.

"A broom?"

"A quarterstaff," he said. "Well, at least it'll do for now. We'll get you something better when we have time."

Miles nodded, looking at the shaft of wood with a new perspective. He had fended well with the iron bar, despite the weight of the thing. He should be much nimbler with this. Miles stood, holding the shaft at his side like a guard with a spear. "I'm ready."

They walked out of the inn, and into a scene of sheer horror. People were fleeing for their lives, running in every direction. Dozens of ghouls roamed through the streets. Miles could see that several of them had already found victims. These were hunched over, feeding on the bodies of the fallen. Others were chasing the common folk of Seahaven. The ghouls were all ragged, many with broken limbs and torn flesh. Some moved quickly, others shambled on lame legs. There were a few that had the preserved look of the one he saw two nights ago, but many more had the look of fresh corpses. For many of them, the only sign of how they had died was a large slash across their throat. Some had knives or other weapons attached to their arms; tied, bolted, or stitched into place. Others looked pieced together from several bodies, such as one with muscled arms sewn onto a thin body. The scene was grotesque, and Miles froze in the doorway.

Gareth stood next to him, his obsidian sword in hand. "No time to waste. Are you sure you are up to this? You could stay here with Nikolai."

Miles thought for a moment. The horrible melee in the streets had shocked him. Who knew what sort of nightmare awaited them in the tunnels beneath the shanty? He was the only one, though, that knew where it was. "You need me," he said, feigning confidence. "Let's go."

* * *

Fergus stood amid the carnage, swinging his huge hammer back and forth as if it weighed nothing. A ghoul lurched at him, and he struck it in the temple. The thing's neck snapped, its head folding over to rest on one shoulder. Still, it came. He pummeled at it again and again, until finally it was an unmoving mass of broken flesh at his feet. Nearby, Filian danced through the throng. His twin blades flashed out in a swirl of deadly grace. He knew he could not fell the monsters with his humble weapons, so he sought to cripple them. His knives slashed through muscle and tendon, rendering arms and legs limp and useless.

Filian's mob had spread out and were working their way through the harbor district towards Shanty Town. In groups of two or three, they separated and took to clearing different streets. The pirate with the two hatchets hacked through the ghouls with an inhuman ferocity, while the old soldier with the bardiche cleaved any dead man before him nearly in two with the heavy poleaxe. Sabers sung through the night air, slicing this way and that. Out of the corner of his eye, Filian could have sworn he saw a pack of children attacking one of the ghouls. He looked more closely, and a small girl with golden locks smiled at him with dead flesh stuck to a knife in her hand.

"Die already!" Fergus roared as he hammered at another ghoul.

"They're already dead, you big oaf," Filian said nearby, startled back to the task at hand by the big man's shout.

"Die again!" Fergus yelled as the hammer fell.

*   *   *

Miles and Gareth made their way through the harbor, carefully avoiding confrontation where they could. They came face to face with one of the creatures and dispatched it with relative ease. Miles struck out with the staff, crippling the thing's knee. As it tried to regain its feet, Gareth decapitated it in one stroke, then set about removing the arms and legs. The disembodied limbs still writhed on the ground as they moved on.

They soon were in Old Town, and Miles tried to retrace his steps from the night before. The cacophony of the battle faded behind them as they made their way, but still they could hear screaming and shouting. Fires were lighting up in parts of Shanty Town, and the sky took on an angry red glow. Miles pointed it out, "The ghouls are burning Shanty Town!"

Gareth looked, then shook his head. "No, I don't think so. Remember, Nikolai said they were mindless. Most likely, we started the fires."

"*We?*"

"Humans. Shanty Towners. Maybe even the guards. In all the chaos, I'm sure people will riot. Anybody with a grudge will take advantage of the confusion to act on it. People who might have been decent to each other before tonight will turn to their baser instincts in the face of such horror," Gareth explained.

Miles didn't understand. "But, why?"

"Human nature," Gareth said, then motioned for Miles to keep moving.

They passed the old cemetery and weaved through one crumbling ruin after another. Miles kept close to the bluff, like the man had the night before. He didn't know how far the shanty he was looking for was, but he knew it would be against the hill that led to the cliffs. Finally, the broken stones gave way to cracked wood, and they knew they were close to their destination.

"You could just show me the door, then find somewhere to wait this out," Gareth said.

Miles took a moment to consider the offer. He didn't want to go traipsing around some moldy cave in search for another fight, but he felt like he needed to. He didn't want to leave his friend alone, either. He knew Gareth could handle himself. What if he got hurt, though? Miles would blame himself. "No, I'm staying with you."

Then he saw it. Miles ran up to the shanty and threw open the door. Inside was that green rug that belonged in some noble manor, and he knew they had found it.

"This is it?" Gareth asked.

"Yes, this is it," Miles said. He lifted one end of the rug and pulled it back. Underneath was a wood trap door set with an iron ring.

Gareth sheathed his sword and grabbed the ring in both hands, pulling open the door. There was a wood ladder leading down into a tunnel lit by flickering torchlight. Gareth climbed down first, looked around, then motioned for Miles to follow. The tunnel was narrow, barely wide enough for one man and so low that Gareth had to hunch over slightly. Torches were ensconced every twenty feet. The tunnel ran straight at first, but soon curved away under the cliff itself. Gareth drew his sword as he worked his way through the tunnel. They continued for almost a quarter of an hour — until they came to an open chamber. There were other tunnels leading off from it, but they knew they had found what they were looking for.

The floor was littered with severed body parts and there was blood splattered all over. Chains hung from the walls, some still holding captive bodies. A simple table lay in the center of the room covered in all manner of knives, saws, needles, and other tools that a surgeon might use. Off to one side, there was a desk strewn with books and scrolls. Before it was a chair, and in the chair a man.

"I knew somebody would find me," the man said. "When Bertram came huffing in here last night, I knew the fool had led you right to me." The man stood and turned around. He wore simple clothes of brown wool, and a heavy leather apron covered them. Blood stained the apron, which had pockets in front full of more surgical tools. The man was gaunt and appeared to be quite old. He had a simple mustache and long hair that hung loosely about his shoulders. "Poor Bertram. The fool of a man should have just run away, not back here. He's waiting for you, though." The necromancer walked over to one of the bodies chained to the wall and patted it on the arm. Suddenly, the bloody mess moaned and writhed about. Miles recognized the man as the one he had chased here last night. The necromancer unclasped the shackles from Bertram's wrists, and the newly made ghoul rushed towards Miles and Gareth.

*   *   *

"How many are there?" Fergus called out as he felled another ghoul with his hammer.

Filian looked down a side alley to the next street and saw one a sailor he had brought from The Lusty Mermaid. The man collapsed to the ground, three of the monstrosities piling on top of him and tearing him apart with hands and teeth. "Too many."

Fergus grunted as he swung the hammer again. They were halfway through Shanty Town, and still more of the things came. They would need an army to kill them all, but so far, the actual soldiers of Seahaven were not to be found. "Blasted city guard should be here," he said.

"I saw some a few streets back," Filian said as he slid behind another ghoul, slicing the tendons in its ankles and sending it crashing to the ground. "They were running for Baron's Hill like death himself was hot on their tails."

"Figures," Fergus said. He was about to take another swing at the ghoul in front of him, when suddenly there was a flash of movement and the dead man's head flew from its shoulders. The big man swung the hammer anyway, batting the headless body aside. Behind it stood a man, thin and pale. He had the clothes of an aristocrat, complete with ruffled lace, but he held a massive bastard sword in both hands.

"Hector?" Filian asked.

The gaunt, pale man smiled. Two sharp teeth gleamed in the firelight when he did, and a shudder ran up the spines of both Fergus and Filian. In a thick accent, he said, "I thought you might require some... how do you say... assistance?" He turned and dispatched two more of the creatures. Hector swung the massive sword as if it weighed nothing. The pale man twisted and danced as the blade flicked out, seeming to seek out flesh of its own accord. Despite his fevered movements, the man's clothing and hair seemed unnaturally still. Fergus saw other blurs of movement, and all around ghouls were falling to flashing blades that moved almost too fast to see. Other dark figures darted through the throng with the same quickness and grace that Hector had displayed. The shadows themselves seemed to come alive, and Fergus knew they had the army he was asking for.

Fergus and Filian looked at each other, both at a loss for words. Fergus shrugged and smiled. "Well, back to work!"

*   *   *

Miles leaped to one side as the Bertram ghoul rushed them, swinging out with the broken broom handle. He struck the leg of the thing, but missed striking the knee as intended. Gareth slashed out with his sword, taking fingers off an outstretched hand. Bertram moved too fast, though, and crashed into Gareth. The older thief was barreled to the ground, his sword skittering away on the stone floor. He held the ghoul's face with both hands, struggling to keep the chomping teeth from his throat. Bertram's own throat had been sliced open, and the flesh of the gaping wound fluttered as it tried to bite down on its prey.

Swinging the shaft of wood, Miles brought it down upon the dead man repeatedly until the handle cracked and splintered. The impacts did not sway the ghoul at all. Looking around desperately, Miles ran to the table. The necromancer was behind it, smiling in glee as his creation set about the task he'd given it. Seeing Miles running towards him, he flinched in fear, then ran down a tunnel. Miles ignored the older man, instead grabbing a bone saw from the table. He ran to where Gareth still struggled, and he started sawing at the back of Bertram's neck.

The serrated blade sliced easily through the flesh, but little blood was left in the body to escape from this fresh wound. Soon, Miles could feel the teeth digging into bone. He sawed harder, fighting through the putrid smell and the sound of grinding bone. Bertram struggled with Gareth, and although his mentor held the head as still as he could, Miles still struggled to cut through. Finally, there was a loud pop as the saw made its way through the neck bones.

The head in Gareth's hands twisted at the sound, and he pulled with all his might. Flesh tore as he pulled, and since the throat was already sliced open, there was little to keep the head attached to the body. He flung the head across the room, its jaws still biting desperately at the air. The now-headless ghoul continued to claw at Gareth. His hands now free, the thief drew a dagger and set about cutting at the thing. Miles dropped the saw and ran to the obsidian sword. The blade was light, but he was not practiced with such a weapon. Despite his clumsy slashes, he crippled the ghoul in several places.

Gareth pushed the torn body off him and rolled away. It writhed on the ground, struggling to pull itself towards him. They had cut muscle and tendon in so many places, however, that its movements were akin to a fish flopping on the deck of a boat. The older thief got to his feet, and Miles handed him the black sword.

"You did good, thank you," he said, struggling to catch his breath.

"He got away," Miles said.

Gareth looked about the room and seemed to notice for the first time that the necromancer was gone. "Which tunnel?"

Miles pointed, and together they ran. This tunnel was like the first they had come to. As they went farther down the corridor, they splashed into pools of water. Soon, they were sloshing through ankle deep seawater. Ahead, the tunnel lie in darkness, and they could see freshly snuffed torches floating in the pools. "He's trying to hide in the darkness," Gareth said.

They both grabbed torches, and on they went. They must have been directly under the castle by now, and a strange feeling of dread overcame Miles. *What if Duke Ravencrest was involved?* he thought.

Gareth held out a hand to stop Miles. They had reached a small chamber, and from here five other tunnels branched off. They were all flooded, and the water surged gently up and down. Somewhere, one or more of them must have led out to the sea. The waves were pushing the water into the tunnels, and it was receding when they did. There was no way to know which way the necromancer had gone.

Chapter Ten

In the month since the night of the ghouls, things had been quiet in Seahaven. Fergus, Filian, and the other fighters from The Lusty Mermaid had put down most of the things with the help of Hector and his kind. The rioting had continued into the next day and through the night, but eventually the city guard showed in force and restored order. Many people cried out about how they did not defend them from the attacks. Even more did not understand the nature of the attacks. The

Council of Barons posted notices and hired criers to walk the streets, shouting the story of how a riot in Shanty Town got out of control. The story was that the common folk turned on each other, and that the killings were a result of the riots.

Miles knew better, as did others. He wanted to speak out, but Gareth cautioned him. *"There are a lot of secrets in Seahaven,"* he had said, *"and there are even more people who would kill to keep them secret."* Gareth had arranged for him to spend time with Nikolai, as well. His reading lessons were advancing rapidly, and the foreign scholar complimented Miles on his quick mind. He learned of some of those secrets in the shadows. He now knew what a vampire was, and more of how ghouls were made. He heard of other terrors in the night; many things he had never imagined. Others, like sirens of the sea, he had thought were legends but now learned were real.

He ran a hand through his curly blond hair, scratching at his head. A few days ago, he was just another homeless child stealing food to survive. He had wanted to become a master thief, like Gareth. The man was more than he seemed, though, and now Miles was involved in these shadowy conspiracies that rippled just under the surface of the city like a shark ready to gobble up its prey.

Miles sighed, resigning himself to the fact that life would never be the same. All he could do, Gareth had told him, was to keep on living until somebody stopped him. It was a morbid thought, but in the end, it was all about taking advantage of the time you had. One never knew when that time would end. Shayla may or may not be weaving his thread into the tapestry of fate, and either way he didn't know when it would be cut short. So, he could do naught but try to make the best of it. He looked up at the plastered building above, to a window over a small balcony. He had set out to do something, and he was wasting time reminiscing.

Miles slung the lovingly carved quarterstaff he held over his back, a leather strap over one shoulder holding it in place. He climbed up an ivy-covered trellis and pulled himself onto the balcony. The window to the small room opened easily, and he slipped inside. Back to work, Miles thought to himself. Padding through the dark room, he peered over the snoring man in the bed. The rasping breaths were deep and loud, and he was sure the man was truly asleep. He looked hard around the room, analyzing every possible hiding place. He ran hands along boards, tugging at a loose one here or there to see if it would pop free. He opened drawers and trunks, rummaging through the contents. Still, he found nothing of interest or value. He opened two wood doors on the front of a simple wardrobe. It contained nice clothing, but nothing that would fit him. There were boots piled up in the bottom. He sighed again.

"Defeat," he said to himself softly. Then he cocked his head to the side in thought. *Feet?*

Crouching down, Miles quietly pulled the boots from the bottom of the wardrobe and set them aside. Feeling carefully along the bottom of it, he found grooves where he did not expect to. He slid his dirk into one of them and slowly pried up a loose board from the bottom. Smiling, he set the board aside and reached into a small space beneath the wardrobe. His hands came back with a small wood box. He opened the box and lit a match from a small tinder kit in his coat pocket. He saw a small bag, two journals, and a folded piece of parchment inside the box. He lifted the bag, which was heavy with coin, and set it aside. He picked up the parchment and held the match over it. It shocked him to see his own name scrawled on the folded paper.

Miles looked around nervously. The heavyset merchant still slumbered in his bed, and no other soul was present. Miles unfolded the note. Gareth had signed it, and read simply: *What took you so long?*

The end, for now…

Not long ago…

"Well," Fergus started, "that's a long story. I was in the crew of a man called Jacobson. His ship, the Bloody Wench, was the terror of the Eastern Sea."

Gareth cleared his throat loudly. "Fergus, that is a long story. Maybe another time?"

Fergus frowned. "Fine, then. I won't spoil it for you, young Miles. We'll just have to wait for another time to tell that tale. Trust me, though, it's a good one."

And now, it is time for Fergus to tell his tale in
The Giant and the Fishes…

Fergus always dreamed of sailing out to sea, but he never thought he would get the chance… until tragedy befalls his family. Suddenly thrust into a world of violence, adventure, and coin, Fergus lives the life he always wanted as a pirate—but he is haunted by his past. As the shadows behind him grow ever darker, the challenges ahead swell like a furious storm.

Continue reading on the next page for a special preview of the first chapter of *The Giant and the Fishes*!

The Giant
and the Fishes

Chapter One

Seahaven wasn't a terrible place to live. At least, I didn't think so. I grew up there, and was always the biggest kid on the street. Never found many problems I couldn't punch my way out of. — Fergus Tomason

Sweat beaded up on Fergus' brow as he pumped the bellows. The heat from the forge was intense. That, plus the weather, made for a miserable day. The air was heavy with humidity and salt, punctuated by the spring heat. The past winter had been a mild one, and it seemed like Seahaven was skipping right to summertime. This was Fergus' sixteenth spring, and he would swear that it was the hottest one yet. But the big lad leaned into his work, shoulders and arms already rippling with tight muscles. He was taller than the blacksmith he worked for, Tomas, who also happened to be his father. Working outside had bronzed his skin, and he already had short, dark hair sprouting on his face and chest. An uncut mop of dark strands crowned his head. He couldn't wait to grow in a proper beard, although the heat made him think twice about it.

Tomas walked over to the forge and shoved a block of iron into it, held with a long pair of tongs. Fergus renewed his pumping, driving air into the forge to heat the metal. He wasn't sure what pa was making today. Probably horseshoes, or nails, or something else equally as boring. Life would be much more interesting had he been the son of an armorer, swordsmith, or gunsmith. As it was, he was the son of a regular old blacksmith. He didn't mind his life. He had a bed, a full stomach, and honest work to keep him busy. He knew that there were plenty of orphan children on the streets who couldn't say the same, like his friend Gareth. The boy wasn't even thirteen years old, but already he could tell that one was a survivor. He was a sneaky one, too. Gareth was always slipping through the shadows, spying, and stealing. That wasn't the way for Fergus, though. He was happy with his work, even if it bored him.

Sure, he had problems, but didn't everybody? Nobody was wealthy in Seahaven, except for the fancypants nobles. Everybody scraped by as well as they could, just like him and pa. It seemed at times it was just the two of them against the world. Fergus never knew his ma, since she died when he was born. They said he was such a big baby, he almost punched his way out of her belly. He would laugh at that, but inside he had always felt guilty about her death. But Tomas didn't seem to hold it against him. He was a grounded man, and he had known the dangers of childbirth before that night. When it came up, he would just say, *"That sort of thing happens all the time. No reason it should be surprising."*

Still, Fergus felt bad, and he tried to do his best to help pa out. Working in the smithy was just one thing he did. He also kept the house up as best he could. And he tried to stay out of trouble, but that wasn't always easy. They say big men have small tempers, and Fergus was no exception to that rule. It wouldn't take much, and he'd be on top of some smart-mouthed brat, bashing his teeth out. That sort of thing wasn't rare for boys his age, but he was a rare boy. His size and strength were his greatest assets, but they usually got him into more trouble than he wanted. A simple scrap in an alley could easily turn into a murder if he wasn't careful, especially with his temper.

Tomas took the ingot of iron from the furnace and carried it to the anvil in the center of the open-air workshop. They were under a shingled roof held up with timber beams. This attached to a two-story plank cottage that served as storeroom, showroom, and home for the two of them. Tomas banged at the iron ingot, flattening it. He turned it and hammered again, stretching the red-hot metal out. Fergus rested for a moment, leaning on the handle of the bellows, and watched his father as he worked. The man deftly shaped what started as a crude chunk of iron into a slender bar. He then set it over the horn of the anvil and started to shape a curve into it. Yes, today it was going to be horseshoes. Fergus pumped the bellows a few more times, and as he anticipated, Tomas brought the curved metal over to heat it again. Thus, did the process continue for most of the day. One after another, Tomas formed chunks of iron into horseshoes as Fergus pumped the bellows and stoked the fires.

Soon, the sun was descending over Baron's Hill—where noble estates loomed over the rest of the city. The main gates were on the other side of the Noble Quarter that sat atop the hill, the only portal through the wall that curved to connect with two towering bluffs. A stone structure stood atop each bluff. On one, an ancient lighthouse. On the other, Castle Ravencrest. The castle was where Duke Piotr and the rest of the Ravencrest family resided, but nobody saw much of them. Here in Shanty Town, nobody could care much if they existed at all. The maze of timber shacks that housed both homes and businesses made up much of the city, bordered on one side by the Mercantile District, and on the other, the harbor. Baron's Hill laid beyond the Mercantile District, and Bleakstone Bay rested beyond the harbor.

Fergus enjoyed going to the harbor when he had the spare time. The air seemed cleaner there, although some would argue that there was nothing clean about the smell of the sea. He marveled at the tall ships, their masts reaching towards the sky. The freedom those men had once they set out to sea was like something from a fable, and Fergus envied them the luxury. Looking at the ships from the dock was as close as he would ever get to that life, though. He would be here, pumping the bellows, until pa let him swing the hammer. Already, he was learning the basics. This was his life, and there wasn't much chance of that changing.

"I think that's enough for today," Tomas said as he wiped sweat from his brow with a linen cloth.

Fergus dropped the handle of the bellows and sighed with relief. He walked over to the water barrel and leaned over it, dunking his head inside. The tepid water felt cool compared to the heat in the air, and he stayed down longer than he should have. As Fergus lifted his head up, a spray of water flew from his hair and sparkled in the evening sunlight. He shook his head and took a deep breath, letting rivulets of sweat and water drip down his bare chest.

Tomas laughed, used to the sight but still amused by it. "You staying for supper, boy? Or are you going roaming?"

"I think I'll head over to the harbor and get some fresh air," Fergus said.

"Fresh? Don't know where you get that notion. You always come back smelling of fish." Tomas reached into a pocket in his apron and tossed a few copper coins to Fergus. "While you're coming back smelling of fish, might as well bring some of the slimy bastards back with you for the pantry."

Fergus smiled and nodded, then made his way quickly out of the workshop before his pa changed his mind. He ran through the twisting streets of packed dirt, weaving between merchant carts and pedestrians. The bare soil gave way to wood plank walkways as he reached the harbor. The land sloped down into Bleakstone Bay here, and tier upon tier of boardwalk twisted down the bluff to the waters below. The tall masts of ships loomed over him; their sails furled while they were docked in port. Men moved back and forth across these boardwalks, pushing carts full of fish, hauling crates, or rolling barrels. All sorts of trade happened here. Almost everything that came into or left Seahaven did so by sea, whether or not it was legal. At the top of the bluff, overlooking the harbor itself, was a press of warehouses and taverns. The goods from the ships needed to be stored somewhere, and the thirsty sailors that did the loading needed to drink. Chief among these, leaning out over the waters under the cliff that held the lighthouse, was The Lusty Mermaid. The sign over the door depicted the namesake creature of myth, cradling an ample bosom in her hands.

Fergus was still young for that kind of place, but there was plenty else to see and do in the harbor. He managed to get himself some watered-down rum for a copper bit and sat on one of the piers watching the sailors do their work. The ships bobbed and swayed in the gentle surf of the bay, the natural feature that had made Seahaven such a successful port. Flags of many nations flew above the ships. Some of them were of foreign make, such as the triangle-sailed caravels from the southern lands of the Hessian Empire. The men from these ships—dark-skinned with tight, curly hair—were all skilled warriors as well as accomplished seamen. With bright-colored clothes and curved scimitars sheathed under silk sashes, seeing a crew of Hessian's was always a treat. There was also a galley from Borska in the north, full of bearded men wearing fur clothing far too warm for the spring heat. They, too, were a fearsome lot, with tempers as short as their axes were sharp. There was much to see in the harbor, and Fergus did not regret spending his free time here in the cool sea breeze. As the sun dipped under Baron's Hill, Fergus haggled with a fishmonger over the price of some salted cod, then made his way back home.

The streets were quiet as darkness descended over Seahaven. The taverns would be bustling now, but most decent folk were settling in for a night's sleep. The morrow would bring an early spring sun and the work would begin again, just like it did every day.

Torches and lanterns lit the streets well enough, but there were still shadows around every corner to be wary of. Fergus' eyes darted left and right as he walked. He may have been a simple lad, but he wasn't a foolish one.

Fergus pushed open the door to the blacksmith shop, calling out as he entered, "Pa, I'm home." There was no answer. Looking around, he saw that the place was in disarray. Someone had tossed and scattered tools, horseshoes, nails, and other wares all over. They'd broken shelves and the small table in the middle of the room. "Pa?" he cried out. He ran to the workshop outside, but the scene there was a similar one of chaos with nobody present. In the back storeroom, fish and grain spilled onto the floor from broken crates in front of their humble hearth. *Dammit, pa. Where are you?*

Upstairs he ran, dropping the burlap sack of cod as he went. His feet pounded on the wooden boards as breath rushed into his lungs. He took the steps two at a time, but still it felt like forever passed by while he climbed. There was a single room on the small second level. There were two beds, a stone basin for water, and two chests for their clothing. Lying in the middle of the floor in a pool of blood was Tomas. His shirt was torn and bloody, and it looked like he had been stabbed several times. Fergus fell to his knees over his father's body, clutching Tomas to his chest as he let out a scream of anguish that sounded like the wail of a banshee.

About the Author

B.K. Bass is the author of over a dozen works of science fiction, fantasy, and horror inspired by the pulp fiction magazines of the early 20th century and classic speculative fiction. He is a student of history with a particular focus on the ancient, classical, and medieval eras. B.K. has a lifetime of experience with a specialization in business management and human relations and served in the U.S. Army as a Nuclear, Chemical, and Biological Operations Specialist. When B.K. isn't dreaming up new worlds to explore, he spends his time as a bookworm, film buff, strategy gamer, and caretaker to an unusual number of cats and one small dog who thinks she's a cat.

Find out more and connect with B.K. at https://bkbass.com

Find *The Giant and the Fishes* at bkbass.com!